In Heaven and Hell

Book 1

by Killjoy Johnson

In Heaven and Hell

CONTENTS

CHAPTER 1
DEATH 💀

Life is short and fleeting for most... just as we realize how fragile it is, we get it taken away from us. Death is inevitable, and though you can fight it, death will ultimately win. Family, Friends, wife, husband, even the children... none are spared from the grim reaper's wrath. All we are is dust in the wind.

The Grim Reaper looms menacingly, its black robes billowing in an eerie wind. Its scythe sparkles in the twilight as it reaps with merciless finality, cutting down kings, queens, and paupers alike. The air of inevitability hangs heavy in the stillness, and you realize that no matter how powerful you are, no one can escape death's icy embrace.

Maki was an unusual child with a unique background. His mother, Towa, was Japanese, and his father, Matthew, was of African American descent. He had been born in the U.S. while she was visiting colleges and decided to stay there. His features approached Japanese standards of beauty but not quite.

Maki's skin was the color of milk chocolate, and his eyes were as black as onyx. His mother embraced his African American heritage with pride; however, she could not fully reconcile herself to raising a child without her family's involvement. But then things took a turn for the worse when Maki was diagnosed with brain cancer.

Towa frantically scrambled to find a way to save her

son. With desperation driving her every move, the scientist worked long and hard into the night, searching for a cure that would rid her child of his deadly brain cancer, even taking her brother Kenshin's assistance in hopes of gaining a breakthrough discovery. But no matter how many experiments she conducted or theories she tested, nothing worked, and each failure was another reminder of how powerless she was. Until one night, she got an anonymous email.

The hairs on the back of her neck stood on end as she opened the anonymous email. The contents contained a map with mysterious, winding lines and three words that sent shivers down her spine: 'The river Styx.' A cold chill ran through her body as she realized what awaited her when she followed the directions. It led her to the Greek island of Crete, a small cave with green glowing algae on the walls.

She followed the sound of running waters deeper and deeper in until she found it. The Waters of the River Styx. She got her samples of the River and headed back, praying that this canister holds the key to healing her baby boy. She gets back to the lab, and her brother Kenshin is furious she would just leave in such a manner, but she explains to him it was indeed an emergency and shows him the liquid.

He's taken back at first because, to him, it looks like ordinary water, but once they throw it under a microscope, the enzymes and microbes in the water tell a different story. Kenshin needed some time to study the water, but Towa didn't have time for clinical trials as her son was dying. As they spoke, every moment counted as she took the liquid to the hospital to cure Maki. She ran upstairs to his room and wasted no time pulling out a syringe and the river waters and injecting it into her son. And as if he was waking from a dream, he opened his eyes. He said, "Hi, Mommy," as the cancer had been completely destroyed. he was safe, but little did Towa know the path she'd put forth in front of her son, a path of pain, suffering, and battle in which no mere mortal could possibly withstand.

And so, Maki went to school like any other kid and tried to make friends, but he felt lonely and isolated once he started middle school. Like many biracial children, he looked different than either race and was bullied for it. But his father, Matthew, had a plan to help his son Maki. He enrolled him in peewee football, so he played for years under the loving guidance of his father, the team coach. Maki was strong, fast, and durable, perfect for football.

Maki had just scored the winning goal for his middle school football team. He was ecstatic as he ran towards his parents and little sister, who were cheering for him from the stands. He hugged them and thanked them for their support. They were so proud of him and his talent.

They decided to celebrate by going to his favorite pizza place. They got into their car and drove away, chatting happily about the game and Maki's future plans. Maki was thinking about how lucky he was to have such a loving family and a bright future ahead of him.

Suddenly, a loud screech pierced the air. A drunk driver had run a red light and crashed into their car at full speed. The impact was devastating. Maki felt a sharp pain in his chest, and then everything went black. He awoke with the car upside down and trapped inside with gasoline leaking in. He called for his father but got no response. He was afraid and didn't know what to do. He started to pray, but no one answered his prayers as the gasoline covered his body. Just then, he heard footsteps. Who's there? He yelled, but to no response; then he heard a lighter flicking. "Oh my God," he thought to himself as the lighter hit the ground and sparked the gasoline. There he sat for hours, burning but not dying, breathing in flames into his lungs and screaming in pain hour after hour until the car was finally burnt to a melted heap of metal.

He woke up in a hospital bed, surrounded by

beeping machines and tubes. He tried to move, but he couldn't. He felt numb and weak. He looked around and saw a nurse standing next to him. She smiled sadly and said, "You're awake. You've been in a coma for two weeks. You had a severe head injury and a broken spine. You're lucky to be alive."

Maki felt a surge of fear and confusion. He asked, "Where are my parents? Where is my sister?" The nurse's smile faded, and she looked away. She said, "I'm sorry, Maki. They didn't make it. They died on the spot. You're the only survivor."

Maki felt a wave of grief and disbelief wash over him. He couldn't believe what he had just heard. He had lost everything in a matter of seconds. He started to cry and scream, "No, no, no! This can't be true! This can't be happening! Please, tell me this is a nightmare! Please, wake me up!"

The nurse tried to calm him down, but he was inconsolable. He wished he had died too. He wished he had never played that game. He wished he had never been born. He wished he could see his family again. He wished he could turn back time and change everything

But he couldn't. He was alone. He was broken. He was alive. Just then, Maki slowly sat up, surprising the nurses and doctors in the hospital. He was fully healed, and his recovery shocked and amazed the doctors. They wanted to conduct tests on him, but Maki was ready to leave the hospital, but to go where…he knew of no family or friends to go see.

 Just then, a man in a grey suit came to his room. His name was Agent Harris from the CIA, and he was there to get Maki to leave with him. He told Maki he wasn't like other teenagers. He had a secret that he could never share with anyone. He was immortal. He didn't know how or why he was immortal but knew the key was within his very blood, and if the wrong people were to get their hands on him, it would mean brutal experiments and torture.

He said if he didn't come with him, he'd always be on the run, looking over his shoulder and wondering if he would ever find someone like him. "Come with me, and I'll take you to a place where you can train to master your abilities; we can teach you to defend yourself from whoever or whatever may come at you." Said, Agent Harris

"Why should I trust you?" Maki asked.

"Who else is there, kid?" exclaimed Agent Harris.

An older Japanese man walked in, saying," Maki, my boy, I'm so relieved to see you alive. Don't tell me you don't remember me." Uncle Kenshin had returned to collect Maki and take him back to Japan with him. Seeing as Maki was just 13 years old and had no other living relatives, he had no choice but to go with Kenshin… a decision he would regret.

CHAPTER 2
UNCLE KENSHIN

After leaving the hospital, Uncle Kenshin and Maki made their way to the airport. "Aren't we going back to my house to get my stuff?" asked Maki

"I'll buy you knew stuff. Just come on." KENSHIN said with a stern voice. As they were leaving, Agent Harris said, "Here, take my card, Maki, just in case you need me."

He took the card and put it in his pocket. They were going straight to the airport to head to Japan to live. Uncle Kenshin and Maki flew from the United States to Japan. They went to his mansion, which was currently empty except for the resident butler and a few security guards hiding. He surprised him with a trip to the basement, where he had set up a dungeon complete with flowery wallpaper and velvet drapes adorning the walls. He was shocked when he saw all the whips hanging on hooks on the wall.

"This is your room, boy," Kenshin said cruelly. He pushed Maki in and locked the door behind him, trapping him in.

"Get used to your surroundings, boy…you'll be here for a long time." The first testing session is in the morning. Be ready, boy."

He had Maki completely imprisoned in the underground dungeon and could not escape. Day after day, he was a living guinea pig, subjected to excruciating tests to uncover the secret of his immortality. Abominable experiments pushed his body to its outer bounds, electrified on Monday, drowned on Tuesday, corrosive baths on Wednesday, and animals unleashed on Thurs to viciously maul him and witness how quickly he healed; Fridays were a special day for it was fry day as he would be exposed to high levels of radiation for hours. Ice spikes plunged into his flesh on Saturday, and on Sunday, he was injected with every poisonous compound known to man.

Maki was pushed far beyond what any man, let alone a child, should be. He suffered night and day for months, but with every experience, his body adapted to the onslaught. Like tempered steel, his body took each attempt at murder as a new challenge to overcome, and each day, he planned his escape from the basement dungeon. Maki could feel his muscles getting stronger each day, his body changing from the constant onslaught of damage and healing from his wounds. Kenshin had no idea of the power that would accumulate within Maki's immortal form as he endured each experience. His strength grew exponentially until, one day, his body was strong enough to break through even the toughest of chains.

Maki's mind was honed like a finely sharpened blade, and he discovered he could access a hidden power within - the ability to move things with his thoughts. With newfound strength, he snapped the chains that had held him captive and burst out of the dungeon into the blazing sun. There stood Kenshin, waiting for him in the courtyard. "Where do you think you're going?" Kenshin asked coolly. Maki steadied himself and replied through gritted teeth, "I'm done with your experiments. I'm done with this dungeon. And I'm done with you!" He charged forward, ready to fight.

Maki's eyes blazed with fury as he launched his body forward to exact revenge on his uncle. But as he unleashed a flurry of punches and kicks, Kenshin remained unmoved, taking each hit with an eerie lack of emotion. With one final spin kick to the head, Maki exposed the wires and circuits lurking beneath Kenshin's skin. At that moment, Maki knew this was not his uncle but an android created to protect him from harm.

"What's wrong, boy?" said a voice from somewhere unseen. "Not what you expected? Where are you, you son of a bitch?!" Maki roared in rage, trembling with anger.

"Near enough to observe your incredible abilities, I can only stand in awe of what you are capable of. But nothing compares to how I feel when I see what you have become."

"Uncle, why? You are the last surviving member of my family - why would you put me through this torture?" Maki asked with sadness in his heart. Science, my boy...your blood is the key to immortality, and I will stop at nothing to ensure it is mine! Even if it means descending into eternal damnation." Kenshin exclaimed. And if ...no, when I find it, hell won't be an issue now, will it?

Maki kicked the severed head of the android and proclaimed to Kenshin, "If you want this power, you'll have to kill me first, and we both know that's not happening any time soon, uncle." I'll be laughing at your funeral, old man. Your legacy will be erased from the annals of history, and I will ensure it. No one will shed a tear at your passing, for you will die in the darkness that you have crafted for yourself, alone and filled with fear. I'll remain here as you suffer in torment, a twisted smirk on my face as I laugh with glee."

Kenshin's eyes flashed with fury as his voice  seethed with hatred. "I will be immortal, boy...and you will be my door to eternal life, but before that, you'll pay for disrespecting your favorite uncle with pain because you must learn your place, boy." As soon as the words escaped his mouth, a pack of cybernetic dogs came around the corner, and Kenshin sneered, "What do you think of my cyber hounds...I built them for the military, but they said it was too inhumane to unleash them on human beings...oh well. Let's see how you do against them."

Maki looked at the vicious dogs with pity and did not retreat. Lifting his chin defiantly, he declared, "What had you done to these poor puppies? I won't accept this any longer!" His telekinesis surged within him, and with one wave of his hand, Maki sent the cybernetic dogs crashing into the far wall. Shreds of robotic metal flew everywhere as he stood tall amidst the carnage. Is that it, uncle? No wonder the military said no...." His voice trailed off threateningly as he glared at Kenshin with a boldness that belied his age. "Bastard!!!" Kenshin screamed as he watched his creations easily dismantled. "This isn't over, boy!! I will make you suffer."

"Save it for supervillain 1.0.1, uncle; sounding like a wannabe Lex Luthor, "Maki said, laughing. The ground beneath Maki trembled and shook, fissures snaking across the soil as something huge lurched out of its hidden depths—a giant robotic arm with razor-sharp claws, gleaming beacons of destruction that scanned the horizon for victims.

"Oh no...it can't be! Seriously, Uncle, a giant robot? What is this an anime?" laughed Maki.

"Oh no, nephew, it's not an anime; it's a horror movie, and you're the star."

The robot revealed its ultimate weapon, its trump card, aiming a large particle cannon at the boy.

"Back to your room, boy," it said in a mechanical grating voice - or else!

 "Or else what?" Said Maki as he stood his ground defiantly; he knew he had to act fast before the robot could unleash its power upon him. He clenched his fists and channeled his telekinetic energy through them, blasting a massive hole into the robot's armor as it attempted to strike. With one shuddering gasp, its lights dimmed, and it lay still.

"Now, where are you, old man?" Maki said with anger in his voice. Come out before I come to find you.

I think I've had enough fun with you today, but ultimately, I will get what I want from you no matter how long it takes; I will figure you out and have my prize. Whatever, next time I see you, I will kill you, Uncle, just know that much......and with that, it went quiet. Kenshin had left, and Maki was alone again, but he was free...he looked out over the setting sun and contemplated his future.

CHAPTER 3
FRIENDS

Maki broke away from the confines of the mansion he had once called home and now found himself in a strange land with no money, family, or friends to turn to. As desperation set in, his heart sank lower and lower until he finally felt a glimmer of hope when he reached into his pocket and pulled out the card Agent Harris had given him. He quickly asked an elderly woman for her cell phone so that he could call Agent Harris. Without hesitation, she complied, and Maki breathed a sigh of relief as Harris told him everything would be alright and he'd take care of all the arrangements for Maki's flight back to America. Suddenly, without realizing it, Maki thanked the woman in perfect Japanese before giving her back her phone and walking off into the unknown with newfound determination.

Maki wandered the streets of Japan in a daze, admiring the sights, but lost his whereabouts. He steeled himself and walked inside a restaurant, only to find that he could comprehend every sign and word written on the walls - as if it were his native tongue. Startled by this revelation, he was then approached by the hostess, who asked him if he had gotten lost speaking fluent Japanese. Maki responded in kind, feeling an incredible power surge rising within him. When she told him where he was, Kyoto, Japan, his eyes widened with wonderment and fear. A whirlwind of questions raced through his mind - What else can I do? Could it be true? Could I fly now, too? That last one might be a little bit farfetched, but who knows?

Maki eyed Agent Harris warily as he asked if he was ready to go home. No, he thought, what exactly am I going back to? His family is dead, and his home lies in ruins, empty of the life that used to be there. He had no choice but to start anew here. He had everything he needed—financial security from his parent's life insurance, a place in Kyoto, and all the anime a person could wish for! At that moment, Maki knew this was it. He was starting a new life in Japan.

Starting school wasn't easy for Maki, as he was bullied for being a foreigner. Agent Harris had left the country, leaving Maki alone. One day, when a group of kids tried to jump Maki, a white-haired boy named Shin stepped in and protected him. Grateful, Maki and Shin became fast best friends, bonding over music and anime.

One day, Maki decided to tell Shin his secret of being immortal. Maki's revelation hung heavy in the air, the words echoing with both disbelief and confusion. To Maki's surprise, Shin merely tilted his head, a spark of excitement igniting his eyes. With a mischievous grin, Shin responded, "Well, Maki, isn't that cool? Because I must confess I come from a long line of exorcists that's been protecting Japan for centuries, and we use the elements to help us defeat our enemies. I can control lightning and wind!" Shin then asked Maki if he knew of anyone else who had powers. Maki exclaimed he didn't, and Shin laughed, saying, "Wait until you come to my place for the holidays."

Maki was confused but intrigued at the concept of meeting others like him who were "enhanced," and so Maki smiled, thinking damn, what a life I'm living. The next day, Shin took Maki to the Yamato family dojo. As they entered, Maki couldn't help but notice the aura of tradition and discipline that filled the air. Shin guided him to where his father, brother, and sister diligently trained. With a great sense of pride, Shin introduced Maki to his father, Sho, a wise and respected martial arts master who had dedicated his life to honing his skills. Maki was in awe of the wisdom and strength exuded by Shin's father. Next, Shin introduced Maki to his brother Ryu, a highly skilled practitioner known for his exceptional techniques. Maki was drawn to the intensity and focus displayed by Shin's brother. Finally, Shin presented his sister Kagome, a graceful and agile warrior with fierce and elegant movements. Maki felt honored to meet such talented individuals and was eager to learn from them in this sacred place of knowledge and tradition. At that moment, Maki knew what he wanted to do with our life; he would become an exorcist like Shin and his family no matter what.

And with that, his training began to be more intense than Maki could ever have imagined. But no matter what they threw at Maki, he endured; he learned  Kung Fu from Shin's father and learned how to control his telekinesis powers from his sister Kagome. He learned how to seal a demon away with mantras and make

15

talismans. He even learned how to use soul weapons, specially equipped weapons for fighting demons, ghouls, and other supernatural creatures.

 Maki felt like a new man, using his powers in combination with the knowledge he'd taken away from the dojo. It was a new day for Maki as he headed out into the world as an exorcist. He was 17 years old and ready for anything… or at least he thought he was… but you can't prepare for some things. In his training, he was taught about all the different types of creatures that lurked in the night.

Maki had always avoided the vampires that lurked in the city's shadows. He knew he was a rare prize for them, an immortal teenager with blood that never ran dry. But one night, he made a fatal mistake. He took a shortcut through a dark alley, where a group of bloodthirsty vampires ambushed him. They dragged him to their lair, where he met the most terrifying creature he had ever seen: the vampire queen. She was beautiful and cruel, with eyes that glowed red and fangs that dripped venom. She claimed Maki as her personal blood bank and tortured him every day with her sadistic games. She drained him of his blood, but he never died. He only felt more pain and despair. He wished for death, but it never came. He wondered if anyone would ever save him from this nightmare.

He did not know Shin, his best friend, was looking for him. Shin had sworn to protect the innocent from the undead ever since he lost his mother to the vampires years ago. He had noticed Maki's disappearance; they summoned a spirit hound to track Maki and traced his scent to the vampire's den. He gathered his family and prepared to storm the place. He vowed to rescue Maki, hoping it was not too late.

By the time they found Maki, his body had been drained of all of his blood, and he was hanging upside down, looking like a dried prune. They cut him down just in time to alert the queen of their meddling; they prepared for battle as Maki lay there shivering and unconscious.

As the vampires descended upon them, Kagome used her ice powers to stop them in their tracks by freezing them in place while Ryu conjured a firestorm to incinerate the undead legions. But to their surprise, the vampire queen wasn't in the lair. It was a trap to kill Shin and his family, knowing they were the only ones who could have stopped her. "We may not have her today, but we won't stop until we get her." said Shin with a confident tone. And so they took Maki back to the dojo to contemplate their next move.

In time, Maki had healed and was ready for revenge. He gathered all the needed equipment and set out to find the vampire queen. They had been tracking the Vampire Queen Victoria for months, following her trail of blood and terror across the country. They finally located her lair in an abandoned mansion on the city's outskirts. They armed themselves with stakes, holy water, and crosses and prepared to face their most dangerous enemy.

They entered the Mansion cautiously, avoiding the traps and guards that Victoria had set up. They made their way to the main hall, where they saw Victoria sitting on a throne of bones, surrounded by her loyal followers. She looked at them with a wicked smile and said, "Welcome, my dear exorcists. I've been expecting you."

Shin and Makai wasted no time and charged at her, hoping to catch her off guard. But Victoria was faster and stronger than they expected. She dodged their attacks with ease and countered with her own. She grabbed Shin by the neck and threw him across the room, crashing into a wall. She then turned to Makai and slashed him with her claws, leaving deep wounds on his chest.

Makai fell to the ground, gasping for air. He saw Shin struggling to get up and knew they had to work together to defeat Victoria. He reached for his cross and held it up, hoping to weaken her. But Victoria laughed and said, "You think that will stop me? I am the Queen of the Vampires, the daughter of Dracula himself. Your pathetic symbols have no power over me."

She grabbed the cross and crushed it in her hand, then threw it away. She moved closer to Makai and said, "You should have stayed away from me, exorcist. You have no idea what you're dealing with. I have lived for centuries and seen and done things you can't even imagine. I have killed thousands of humans, and I will kill thousands more. You are nothing but food to me, and I'm hungry."

She bent down and opened her mouth, ready to bite Makai's neck and drain his life. But before she could, Shin came from behind and stabbed her in the heart with a stake. Victoria screamed in pain and shock and looked at Shin with disbelief. She said, "How...how did you...

But it wasn't enough to finish the Queen as she stood back up, ready for round 2. Just then, an icy gust of wind blew through the mansion as Shin's sister Kagome arrived to assist in the battle. What do I miss? Said Kagome as she called forth a small blizzard to capture the Queen in ice.

Kagome then threw her father's katana shin and said, "Use this to finish her." Shin took the mystical blade in his hands, unsheathing it caused lightning to fill the room. Shin had the power of the gods in his hands. He grabbed the blade and decapitated the queen right then and there. Her icy head rolled onto the ground. Maki fully healed and took the chance to jump into the air and stomp down upon the queen's head, finishing her.

"Feeding time is over bitch." Maki exclaimed as he fell to his knees in exhaustion. They had finished the queen off and was going home, the battle was over, or at least they thought it was… but it was just the beginning.

CHAPTER 4
THE BOUNTY

Meanwhile, a shadowy figure watches as Maki and Shin celebrate their victory against the vampire queen Victoria. "I must inform his highness about this."

The underground city of the cemetery was home to millions of undead immortal creatures such as vampires, ghouls, and other creatures and was ruled by a council of the undead. First, there was Victor the vampire, the Prince and son of Dracula. Then, there was Lilith, the demon lord of the cemetery. And last, there was Enoch, the ghoulish Lord.

At this moment, Victor is enraged by the murder of his sister, Victoria, by the two Japanese exorcists, Maki and Shin. Peace is crucial in their home, the cemetery, but the injustice fills Victor with resentment and rage. Enoch and Lilith, significant figures who value the tranquility of their city, oppose the very thought of war.

"I must have my justice!" declared Victor in a coliseum of his peers.

"My sister must be avenged."

"Your sister was blood-crazed and mad, Victor." said Lilith

"It's a surprise she has lasted this long in the mortal world."

"I don't care what she was doing in the mortal realm; she was of my blood, and my pride will have nothing less than retribution. Justice for Victoria, death to the exorcists! "Victor exclaimed.

The crowd roared around them, "No justice, no peace, no justice, no peace."

Enough!!! Yelled Enoch. "I won't have vigilante justice in my city. The council has voted Victor!"

"If you don't satisfy my bloodlust, then I will, "Victor said under his breath.

To avenge his sister's death and avoid direct conflict, Victor sets a high bounty on the heads of Maki and Shin, thus indirectly inviting chaos to the peaceful cemetery.

He summons the ancient vampires, the Trinity, to hunt down Maki and Shin and return their heads to Victor.

From the shadows, three figures emerged, revealing his assassins.

"Go now…drink as much as you want, but bring me their heads."

Meanwhile, back in the dojo, Maki and Shin are introduced to Sargent Kane, an old war buddy of Shin's father, Sho. He was 6'7" and had a body that looked like it was made from granite.

Behind Sarge were a pair of twin girls looking on curiously at Shin. As the adults talked, the girls just stared at him intensely.

"What?" Shin asked as he became more and more uncomfortable.

"Your hair is white like Snow," they said in unison. "That's so cool"

"Oh, let me introduce my girls," said Sarge, laughing." This is Kimiko, and this is Hariko." The girls bowed their heads and said, "Nice to meet you."

"Ok, I'm going to the store. Who wants what?" Maki asked the room.

"I'm fine, thank you, Maki." said Sho. "May we have some chips, Daddy?" asked the twins in unison. "Sure, why not? As a matter of fact, I'll go with you to get them, Maki." Sarge said while standing up out of his seat.

"I'll go too!" said Shin as he jumped up to get to the door.

And so Sarge Shin and Maki made their way to the convenience store to get snacks, unaware of the dangers that lurked in the night waiting for them.

As darkness of the night enshrouded the town, three fearsome vampires known as the Trinity descended upon Shin, Maki, and Sergeant Kane. With their piercing blood-red eyes and menacing fangs, these unearthly beings exuded an aura of malevolence. Yet, unbeknownst to the vampires, Sergeant Kane possessed unique skills honed through years of rigorous military training. With unwavering determination, Kane engaged the Trinity in a fierce battle, his agility and strength proving to be an unmatched force. As the clash ensued, his calculated strikes swiftly subdued each vampire, leaving them to crumble into nothingness. His comrades, Shin and Maki, watched in awe as their fearless ally single-handedly vanquished the formidable Trinity, leaving no trace of their nefarious presence. In that moment, Kane stood as a symbol of hope and triumph against the darkness threatening their world.

After watching Sarge defeat the Trinity single-handedly, Maki started to wonder if Sarge was also enhanced. "So what else can you do? "Maki asked

Sarge just smiled at him and said, "Let's pray you never have to find out." Maki just stood there bewildered at the response." So, let's get to the store; the kids need their chips." Sarge said with a confident tone. "Sir, yes sir," Shin said as he saluted. "Stop it, bro…. Got you looking like a jackass right now." Maki whispers to Shin.

With the Trinity dead and Shin and Maki safe, the three returned to the Yamato family dojo, unaware of the looming threat that ultimately awaited them.

CHAPTER 5
THE REAPER WARS

Meanwhile, back at the cemetery, the powerful vampire Prince seethed with uncontrollable anger at the failure of his trusted Trinity of vampires. He had sent them on a mission to eliminate Maki and Shin, the formidable warriors from the Yamato family that had proven to be a thorn in his side for far too long. Their survival stung his pride and fueled an insatiable thirst for revenge. Determined to erase this blight, Victor concocted a diabolical plan. Utilizing the mythical Eye of Osiris, an artifact of immense power, he sought the expertise of Kenshin, Maki's treacherous uncle and a vile scientist well-versed in the dark arts. Together, they delved into forbidden realms of necromancy, successfully reanimating the dead. An army of cyborg zombies, known as the Reapers, was born through unholy experimentation. Victor's sole purpose for these abominations was to hunt down and eradicate Maki, Shin, and the entire Yamato family, leaving no remnants of their existence. The stage was set for an epic and explosive showdown that would determine the fate of these supernatural adversaries.

As Victor sets his diabolical plan in motion, back at the Yamato family dojo, Maki and Shin are training diligently with Sarge, attempting to break through their limitations and reach higher strength so that whatever comes their way, they will be ready.

Each of them came at Sarge with everything they had to hit the towering old soldier, but to no avail, for Sarge was just too quick and agile to land a single blow. Even when Shin resorted to using his lightning powers to amplify his speed, he couldn't land a single blow.

'What are you made of?" Maki exclaimed as he sat on the ground, exhausted. "You mean to tell me he's faster than lightning itself?" "Your attacks are predictable and sloppy; I can read you too easily," Sarge said

Meanwhile, as they trained, the twins, Kimiko and Hariko, were setting up the new defense system for the dojo. They set up cameras and their defensive drones all over the city, and using their technopathic powers, they linked up to the system with no problems at all; they could see everything in the city. Kimiko, who had the ability to control software, set up the computer system, and Hariko, who could connect to the hardware, set up the drones to be ready for anything.

Just then, a shadowy figure walks up to the Yamato dojo gates and knocks at the door. Kimiko sees a man standing there and asks, "May I help you?" The older man looks at the camera and asks, "Are Maki and Shin home?" who wants to know?" Asked Kimiko. Just then, a hoard of zombies with blazing red eyes started to walk slowly towards the dojo.

"Tell him Uncle Kenshin says hello." And with that, the cybernetic zombies went into action, leaping through the air and into the dojo's courtyard, looking for flesh.

And with that, the battle had begun as zombies swarmed the Kyoto city streets. They were attacking innocent citizens and anyone unlucky enough to be on the streets that night. In an instant, the twins acted, activating the alarm, alerting the Yamato clan of the dangers awaiting them. "Launch the drones!" Kimiko yelled as the zombies started to scale the walls of the Yamato family shrine, trying to get their way in.

With a loud roar, the drones launched into the air, locking on to the hordes of zombies and decimating hundreds of them at a time, launching rockets and firing specially designed bullets at the swarm.

At that moment, Shin kicks open the Yamato Shine doors to find hundreds of zombies awaiting them; he grabs his katana and takes his stance; the sky blackens, and thunder rings out in the sky. With a loud boom, Shin unsheathes his sword, unleashing the powerful lightning within and instantly cutting down zombie after zombie.

Maki follows suit, grabbing zombies with his telekinesis and flinging them into the Kyoto night sky to be struck down by lightning filling the air. Sarge grabs a pair of power gauntlets and goes to work, smashing the heads of every zombie he sees.

"Where are they all coming from?!" Kagome asks as she shreds through the horde with her ice powers, freezing and then breaking them in the ice. "I don't know, but we can't let up," says Ryu as he blasts the swarm with hellfire. They battled the zombies throughout the night until dawn, never letting them into the dojo's inner sanctum.

As the zombie hoards break through the defensive line of the Yamato clan, Shin's father, Sho, arrives. Riding a lightning bolt. he yells, "Enough!!" He brings thousands of bolts of lightning to the battlefield, incinerating the thousands of remaining zombies all at once. The day was saved... for now.

But for how long was the question... with the unholy alliance of Victor and Maki's uncle Kenshin, how long would our heroes know peace? How long until the next assault... the next attack...Maki then decided it was time to go on the offensive and take the fight to the evil duo. It was time to go to the cemetery and end this...Once and for all.

CHAPTER 6
THE IMMORTAL

In the aftermath of the Yamato family dojo assault, the city of Kyoto was in disarray. Hundreds died in what was called a freak thunderstorm, the deadliest in recorded history. All that was left of the zombie hoard were scorched scraps of metal....no flesh. The smell of death filled the air.

Maki had seen enough. As he gazed at the carnage, he felt great guilt and responsibility for the hundreds of innocent citizens who got caught up in the middle of the war. Their blood was on his hands. He thought of his uncle, and how he could never forgive him for the thousands of people, he must've dammed with his unholy, researching, trapped souls longing for release.

"I must put an end to this." Maki thought to himself.

"I'll have no more death on my watch, even if I must kill to prevent it."

"We found him, Dad...he entered an abandoned mansion on the city's outskirts." Said the twins in unison.

Sarge looks at the screen and nods at the girls with approval. "Well, done, girls, send me the information to my phone."

He said, loading up his weapon. Maki looks and recognizes the house instantly as the very house he was tortured in for all those years. Maki's rage started to build within him as he thought of the abuse he'd suffered at the hands of Kenshin. Finally finishing the old man was all Maki could think of as his powers swelled within him.

The crew packed their gear and headed to the mansion with extermination in mind. They arrived at the house and entered cautiously, aware of their surroundings; deeper and deeper in, they went until they came across an odd door in the basement that wasn't there when Maki was there. They opened the door to find a labyrinth of tombs leading deep underground. They followed the pathway until they saw a large gate in front of them. It was the gateway to the cemetery.

 They had finally reached the gates of the Necropolis, a massive arch of bones and skulls that marked the entrance to the city of the dead. They had seen the dark spires and towers that rose from the ground and the eerie glow that emanated from them. They had heard the moans and screams that filled the air and the clatter of bones and metal that signaled the presence of the undead.

They had taken a deep breath and had stepped into the city, ready to face their destiny.

"Release the drones, girls," Sarge said, and with that, Kimiko and Hariko opened up the large nap sack, releasing hundreds of little bug-sized drones. They swarmed the city in minutes, filling the air.

"Ok, our job is done, girls. It's up to Maki and Shin now," said Sarge, laughing. Meanwhile, Maki started to build up his power in the middle of the cemetery. Calling forth all of his telekinetic powers, he slammed his fist into the ground, causing a large earthquake and shaking the Necropolis to its core. "Kenshin!!!" he yelled. "Come face me!!! Or I'll bring this city down to the ground."

With that, the other cemetery creatures began screaming into the night. "Death to the mortals! Revenge for Queen Victoria!!"

The vampires were ready for war. But just as the vampires descended upon them, Ryu conjured a fire tornado to incinerate the undead legions from a far-off rooftop. Kagome summoned ice from the sky, bombarding the hundreds of vampires before they could descend on Maki.

Kenshin!! Come to me!! Maki exclaimed as he lifted vampires from the crowd and flung them into the night sky.

Shin, now equipped with the ability to control the lightning within him, conjured lightning and wind to create his version of the fire tornado but with wind and lightning. Just then, the twins got their orders to ignite the drones, bringing explosive cataclysms to the streets.

Each drone explodes with the force of a small nuclear device, decimating the Necropolis with every single explosion. War had come to the Necropolis, where peace reigned for hundreds of years.

Just then, three large armored ghouls came forth to stop the chaos. They were Enoch's guards. They descended upon Maki, showering him with hellfire in an attempt to stop the Carnage. But the fires did not affect Maki as he swatted the flames away. He jumped into the air and onto one of the warriors, twisting the head clean off the armored ghoul… then back-flipped off the ghoul, and energy blasted away the others with his mind.

He lifted one of the armored Titans and threw him into a building, bringing the place down with drones to complete the deadly combo attack. Just then, Sarge jumped into the fight, bringing powerful lightning gauntlets ready to incinerate the undead legions. As Sarge arrived, the ghouls arose from the rubble, ready for round 2.

To find your uncle, kid…let the adults get to know each other. Sarge said, laughing at the ghouls in his presence. And who are you? Asked one of the ghouls. "Me? I'm Sargent William Kane, the last person you'll ever see."

As Maki ran off to find his uncle, the ghouls started to chant. They attempted to summon a strong spell to kill Maki in one powerful attack. Just then, Sarge jumped behind Maki. Whatever that is, aim that beauty over here. They looked at each other then, Sarge, and said. "As you wish, mortal."

They aimed at Sarge and fired, blasting a purple and red beam at Sarge, pushing him back and to an abandoned building, destroying everything in its way.

In the aftermath, the twins looked on in horror as the ghouls laughed at the destruction they had caused. Just then, a slight growl could be heard coming from the wreckage. As the smoke cleared, a large white-haired werewolf stood there, teeth glistening in the night.

"My turn now," Sarge said with a blood-curdling roar as he left into action, clawing and biting the ghouls.

With one swing, Sarge had decapitated one of the two remaining ghouls, leaving him to run around headless and confused. He then leaps at the other, mounting him and mauling the ghoul. In moments, Sarge had decimated the duo and was searching for his next victim. "I smell him...all around me is the stench of death... except for one scent! "Using his higher sense of smell, Sarge could find Kenshin no matter where he had hidden himself. Maki follows close as Sarge leaps into the night sky, jumping from rooftop to rooftop in his search for Kenshin.

He dives into an old cathedral, kicking in the doors..." found you," he says maliciously. And there stood Kenshin and Victor in shock at being discovered. "He's all yours, kid," Sarge exclaimed as Maki entered the room.

"Times up, old man," Maki said, grabbing his uncle with telekinesis. It's time to pay for your crimes. And what of your crimes, boy !?" Victor asked.

"You killed thousands of my people today, and you killed my beloved sister Victoria as well... what of your crime? What of my justice?!"

With that, Victor lunges at Maki, but Maki easily dodges and counterattacks, saying.

"To hell with your justice. Your sister was blood-crazed and mad!! She wanted me as a blood bank so she could drink from me forever. So yeah, I killed her dead."

Don't come at me looking for justice when you helped Kenshin kill all those people in Kyoto. I'll make both of you pay for your evil.

And with that, the two fought, Maki stunning the vampire with lefts and rights—the training with Sho and Sarge showing through. Maki had Victor beaten when it came to hand-to-hand combat, but the ancient vampire wasn't out yet.

He jumped out the cathedral window to collect some time to empower the eye of Osiris to do his bidding. Now, boy, it ends for you. I'll make sure you can't come back from this. Then, a giant fireball was conjured in the night sky. It was as bright as the sun but twice as hot.

Victor threw it at Maki, incinerating the cathedral and graveyard surrounding it and leaving a large Crater in its wake, which starts to fill with water from the adjacent river.

Victor, laughing in the sky floating, said. Living immortal, eh?! Ha.

Just then, a figure comes out of the waters. It's Maki having most of his clothes burned off him.

"Was that the best shot you had?" Maki asked

"If so, you'll never be able to kill me."

Just as Victor started to say the chant to hit Maki with another fireball, an ice shard hit him mid-air. "Hey asshole... that's my brother," Shin yelled at Victor as he drew his sword, unleashing lightning and thunder. Fire and then ice hit Victor, keeping him from finishing the incantation. "Sorry, but no way in hell are we gonna sit back and let you throw another one of those." Said Sarge as he tackled Victor to the ground. "Get off me, you damn beast," Victor yells as he knocks Sarge off him.

Just then, thunder could be heard for miles away as Shin took his stance. The lightning accumulates around him as he calls forth the power. It swells within him. He unsheathes it, unleashing lightning onto Victor, electrocuting the vampire Prince and stopping him in his tracks.

Then Sho arrives, puts his hands together, and says, "Time to end this with one final attack." He says some mantras and finishes saying. "Gates of heaven open!!"

With that, an amazing thing happens as a large gate appears in the sky opening and showers Victor with sunlight, incinerating all the vampires of the cemetery in one fell swoop. Leaving only ghouls and other creatures to survive the assault. And with that, it was over. The Yamato clan decimated Victor and the hordes of his bloodthirsty vampires. Now, peace could return to both the living world and the cemetery. But what of Kenshin, who had escaped in the chaos of battle...

I believe that Maki and the Yamato family will be ready if he ever shows his face again.

It ends with Kenshin lurking in the darkness with the eye of Osiris cackling in the night.

CHAPTER 7
PEACE

After Maki and the Yamato clan defeated Victor, they all started to head back home. Just as they were about to exit, they heard a faint cry for help. They followed the sound and found a girl locked in a cage. She was pale and thin, with long black hair and bright green eyes. She wore a red kimono and had a wooden staff by her side.

She introduced herself as Sakura, a blood-bending shrine maiden. She had been kidnapped by Victor, who wanted to use her blood magic for his evil plans. She had been held captive in the cemetery for months and had lost all hope of escape. She begged Maki to free her and take her away from this nightmare.

Maki felt compassion for the girl and decided to help her. He broke the lock on the cage and lifted her in his arms. He carried her out of the cemetery back home, back to freedom.

They brought her to the Yamato family dojo to heal from her ordeal. It took weeks, but in time, Sakura started to feel her strength coming back to her; she told them she used to be a sniper for the military but had to return home and take care of her family shrine after her grandmother passed away. She thanked the Yamato family for their hospitality and vowed to repay them for their kindness. And with that, she returned home. She contacted Kimiko and Hariko, calling her the third twin.

The girls were inseparable, always-on video chat. With Sakura's help, the twins created more advanced creations to prepare for the next ordeal that should arise. They worked with Sakura to create the Slayers. Combined with Sakura's blood magic, mechanical engineering created the perfect cybernetic warriors. They were faster than any vampire, stronger than any ghoul, and resistant to fire, ice, lightning, and most other elemental attacks. Each carried with them an arsenal powerful enough to flatten a country with ease.

With these new androids, the twins felt secure that they'd be okay no matter what they faced.

Meanwhile, Sarge was in the woods training with Sho to control the wild beast within him. "Now, when I say go, you let loose with the fireworks," said Sarge

"Got ya boss." Said Sho, and as soon as Sarge said go, Sho unleashed a flurry of lightning bolts to hit Sarge. But Sarge was too quick, dodging the bolts with backflips and somersaults. Trying to reach a new level of power with his werewolf transformations, he transformed into the beast as he jumped and dodged the bolts, increasing his agility, speed, and strength with each passing moment. As they trained, Sarge asked Sho, "So what are the kids up to? "

"Well, Maki and Shin are visiting my father for further training, and I think my dad will finally make Shin his katana."

"That's great news. He deserves it, and he's earned it," said Sarge, dodging the lightning.

"And I want Maki to learn the dragon style of kung fu. I think it would fit his style of fighting," said Sho. "I remember even you couldn't master that form." Said Sarge

"Yes, but I think Maki can do what I couldn't. Master his soul to master the style," said Sho Confidently.

"Well, with your father teaching him, I can see him breaking through his limitations and reaching that new level," said Sarge.

Meanwhile, back at Sho's father's house, Renjin Sho's father is training Maki to unleash his potential and free his soul. He tells Maki to break through a wall of granite with his powers. But not his mind power but his soul…. Maki, unsure how to do it, uses his telekinesis to break through.

"No," Renjin exclaimed. "Anyone can break stone with force. I want you to do it with will alone. Try again this time, but this time blindfolded." And so, his training commenced under the grueling tutelage of Renjin.

And so, the days turned into weeks, the weeks into months, and months into years, and 7 years had passed in no time. Maki's final test was underway, and the granite wall stood before him. With a thunderous crash, he closed his eyes and broke through the wall.

"Well done, my boy," said Renjin proudly as he watched him in awe. You've done it...your soul and body are finally in perfect harmony.

"I've taught you all I can; the rest is up to you. Now go fly, my boy."

But Maki was a boy no longer. Time had caught up with Maki, and he was a man now, ready to take on the world if need be.

With enhanced strength, speed, and agility, Maki was ready for anything fun the world had in store for him, or at least he thought he was.

Unbeknownst to them, a great evil was stirring on the horizon, ready to test our hero's new resolve. Would they be ready for the impending doom tomorrow had in store?

Deep within the earth, a madman was completing his ultimate creation—a perfect cybernetic warrior. Powered by the eye of Osiris, this creature was leagues past the technology the twins had to offer.

He imbued the beast with the powers of telekinesis, pyrokinesis, cryokinesis, and matter manipulation. He imbued the creature with the ability to absorb the blood and life-force energy out of his victims and add it to his strength.

Kenshin was obsessed with revenge for the

humiliation he suffered at the hands of Maki and the Yamato clan. He designed the android with one purpose: total destruction of Maki and his friends. With his evil technology, he even found a way to extend his life just long enough to get his revenge.

"Now, all that is needed is for the computer to finalize its programming. Then they will all suffer my wrath." Said Kenshin in a diabolical tone. He had programmed the computer with video footage of the Yamato clan and information about Maki and his friends." No surprises this time." said Kenshin. This time, my Reaper Lord will get the job done. He bestowed upon the creature the knowledge of alchemy and magics. Giving him the advantage of mystical powers and an arsenal powerful enough to finish the Yamato family once and for all. "All that's left is the final programming, and he will be free to bring the pain to those bastards up there." Said Kenshin Confidently.

"Soon, my beauty, soon. Soon, you'll have this world begging for mercy, my beautiful Reaper." Said Kenshin.

As Kenshin waited for the programming to finish, he sat down and walked to his lab table. Just then, a loud beeping came from the tube holding his creation. He ran over to see what the commotion was. Just then, a hand broke through the tube, impaling him.

"What....is...this?" He asked, staggered as he lost pints of blood from his chest wound. "What have you done?"

" I kill father.... it's what you made me do, is it not? said the android

"Before you die, please... tell me my name."

"Adam," Kenshin said with his last breath as he lay on the ground bleeding out. "

"Adam. Yes, thank you, father. I like my new name better than my old one."

"Old one? "Asked Kenshin.

"Yes... I remember it was... Victor."

Somehow, the eye of Osiris had retained Victor's soul and memories within the jewel, and now he was reborn.

And with that, Kenshin was dead, but this new threat was active and ready for battle. With the memories of Victor flowing through the android and a new name, he was ready to bring the fight to Maki and the others. Would the Yamato clan be ready for this new threat?

CHAPTER 8
REVENGE

Miles underneath the earth, Adam, Kenshin's final Creation, was active and ready for war with the Yamato clan. He stepped out of the tube and over Kenshin's body. With a robotic voice, he recited a spell, bringing forth water to his feet from the dark abyss.

"Control over the elements, now this is an interesting body." Adam proclaimed as he walked on the water to the stairwell. He hovered over the door and said. It's time as he opened the door to the outside world—the light of the blazing hot sun shining upon the former vampire prince for the first time.

And with a step, he was airborne. Flying through the sky with determination in his blazing red eyes.

Death to Maki, he thought to himself as he flew, going Mach 3 and cutting through buildings and anything else that got in his way. He flew all the way from India back to Japan in minutes. Then, like a hawk hunting his prey, he hovered over Kyoto and watched and waited. He waited for nightfall. He waited for his opportunity to strike, for he didn't just want Maki; he wanted the whole clan dead at his feet. And with this new body, he could do it.

So, Adam watched patiently as Maki shin and the others started to reassemble at the dojo. The twins had gotten an anonymous email saying the dojo was in trouble. So, they called Sarge Maki and the others back, unaware of the cataclysm awaiting them.

As Maki and Shin arrived at the dojo, Kimiko and Hariko yelled, "Hi, big brothers!" as they entered. "Hey, guys. What do we miss?" Asked Sho. "We got this email saying that something was coming, and with our track record, we figured we should bring you guys home." "So, where's this new threat?" Asked Maki

As the words came out of Maki's mouth, Adam recited another spell. This one fills the night sky with dark thunderclouds. "It's time to play," said Adam.

And with that, lightning bolts came crashing down upon the dojo. "What the hell is that?" Is your dad having an issue, bro?!" Maki asked.

"That's not my dad. I can sense my dad, and that's not him."

"Then what the hell?!" Maki asked with fear in his voice.

Just then, Adam came crashing down onto the dojo's roof. He had finally arrived to seek his revenge upon the Yamato clan. He stood up, towering over Maki and his friends—red eyes gleaming in the night.

"Who's first?" He exclaimed as he looked over the

chaos. Maki stood up, asking, "Now, who the fuck are you supposed to be? Santa? That you?"

"Yes, and I've got presents for each of you." Said Adam as he grabbed Maki by the throat. "But you die last. After you witness me kill your friends." Adam said with the intent to have Maki watch as he slaughtered his loved ones. With that, he threw Maki into the wall with such force it broke Maki's spine, leaving him unable to move. He then looked at Hariko as she crouched in the corner of the room. "Scared children have the sweetest blood, "Adam proclaimed as he hovered over to Hariko.

"Not scared, just busy," said Hariko as she revealed the small device in her hands. Just then, a Slayer slams into Adam, pushing him out of the dojo and into the outer courtyard. The Slayer and Adam start to battle as Kagome runs outside to join. She attempts to conjure an ice storm, but Adam is prepared as he throws a stone at Kagome, knocking her out. Just then, a second Slayer jumps into the Frey and a third. That's when Adam looked and realized he was surrounded. He levitated off the ground and started to spin. Then hellfire engulfed him as he started speaking in tongues. Then the fires morphed into fire snakes wrapping around Adam. One Slayer jumps onto Adam but is quickly thrown off. Another attempt was made to blast him with a plasma blast, but it did no damage.

 Just then, Maki comes barreling in wearing a specialized battle suit made by the twins for when he's too injured to fight. It increases his strength and speed by 100-fold. He jumps past the snakes and directly at Adam, punching him out of the air and stomping down on him. He then mounts Adam and delivers a flurry of punches down on him. He jumps away just in time for the Slayers to blast Adam into the crater, seemingly incinerating him, but when the smoke clears, Adam stands unscathed.

Maki then pulled out his plasma blades, which could cut through anything. He jumped in to attack with everything he had, but Adam easily dodged the attacks, kicking him away. Just then, Ryu jumps in with his hellfire sword, unleashing fireballs at Adam, but he swats away the flames with one hand.

"Combo attack," says Maki as he looks at Ryu. Ryu nods his head in agreement. And with that, they jump into action, hitting Adam from all sides with punches, kicks, and slashing with their soul weapons. But no matter how much damage they inflicted, the larger-than-life villain would not fall.

Just then, a shard of ice came crashing on Adam, pinning him down. Kagome had regained consciousness and was pissed off.

"That rock hit me in the face, you son of a bitch!!" yelled Kagome as she held her face. She starts to lower the temperature around Adam to freeze him in place permanently, but just then, Adam starts to chant an incantation that summons a portal above the heads of our heroes. Then, a large grey ghoul lands on the battlefield between Adam and the others. With a roar, he started to attack our heroes, giving Adam time to free himself.

"Enough games," Said Maki as he jumped into the air. And with a flurry of slashes, he dismembered the beast and landed in front of Adam, who was now free. They stood looking at each other. Then, a crackle of thunder fills the air. A lightning bolt strikes Adam from above and then from behind. Shin comes flying in with his new katana in hand. He slashes at Adam, causing the most damage anyone has caused since this all began.

The thunderbolt pushes Adam into Maki, who kicks him through the wall of a building.

"Now I know that hurt him." Says Shin as he stands next to Maki, ready for round 2. "Fuck…" exclaimed Maki as Adam walks out of the rubble. "Who is this guy?!" Using his powers, Maki grabs two dumpsters and slams them into Adam, but he just incinerates the dumpsters with his mind. But as he turns back around, a thunderbolt hits him square in the face, blinding him momentarily, giving Maki the chance to jump into action, and with that, Maki starts the assault on Adam, kicking, punching, and kneeing. But no matter the damage Adam took, it always rose back up. Maki was beginning to get tired. He had hit Adam with all he had. But to no avail. Shin struck him down with lightning bolt after lightning bolt, but none could stop the behemoth. Kagome hits him with an ice beam to freeze him in place, but he walks through the icy blast and almost cuts her down. Ryu jumps in to save her at the last moment.

Thanks, says Kagome, but there is no response. Ryu? She looks at her brother as he bleeds out in her arms. Ryu!!! She yells in agony as she sees Ryu close his eyes, probably for the last time. She screams into the night sky, summoning a blizzard that engulfs the city. "You killed him! You fucking killed my brother!!! You bastard!!" screamed Kagome as she summoned two ice golems to kill Adam. "Go… kill… him… Now!"

As the tears freeze on her cheeks, the ice golems attack Adam. Swinging giant clubs at the villain, attempting to end his life, Adam dodges the attacks easily. Until Maki grabs Adam, holding him in place for the golems to batter them. But just then, Adam recites another spell, turning the golems into stone, throwing Maki into them, and breaking them on contact.

Just then, a blood-curdling howl could be heard piercing the night sky. Just then, a pair of claws break through the earth, grabbing Adam from underneath and dragging him into the abyss.

 It was Sarge in full beast form, and he had dragged Adam into the Subway system to isolate him from the others and have him one-on-one. And so, a mighty battle ensues as Adam punches and kicks, but Sarge is too much for him in the dark as he dodges all of Adams's attacks and counters with his own. Sarge slams him into the walls and smears his face onto the electrified third rail. Clawing and biting, Sarge decimated Adam one-on-one.

As Adam and Sarge battled in the Subway, everyone else huddled around Ryu and tried to save his life. They looked at the wound, and it was deep. He bled out everywhere. Just then, Kimiko Said blood, we need blood magic. Sakura can heal him. Kagome froze the wound so they could move him, and they left looking for Sakura—all exempt Maki, whose rage had built within him.

Master Renjin said never to use dragon style unless it was life or death, and now one of mine is dying because I didn't end this earlier. Enough is enough. Just as the others left, Sarge came out of the subway battered and broken but seemingly victorious. Just then, Adam came up from behind and impaled Sarge through the back.

"Damn dirty dog," says Adam as he drops Sarge to his knees, about to land the killing blow.

"I said enough, "said Maki as he teleported to stop Adam's hand before it landed. A green aura emanates from Maki as he saves Adam from killing Sarge. Maki, using his soul powers, pushes Adam away. "What is this…I have no data on this technique.

"Well, then, let me educate you. This is dragon style. The last thing you'll ever see."

With that, they began to fight, Maki using the style taught him by Renjin, and began to dismantle Adam piece by piece. Starting with hands to the body and face that does damage to him. Then, using his powers, he lifts Adam into the air and volleyballs him around the city. He completely owns Adam at this point, just blocking all of his attacks and smacking him around like an unruly child. He then grabs Adam by the throat and plunges his hand deep into Adams's chest, ripping out the eye of Osiris.

"But I need that." Says, Adam.

"I got what you need right here." Says Maki.

He then kicks Adam into the air and clutches his fist for his final attack. With the power radiating off him, he conjures an energy ball in the fist of his right hand, looks up at Adam, soaring through the air, and fires. The recoil pushed him back a few feet.

As it makes contact with Adam, it explodes, filling the night sky with a green glow that could be seen from space.

And in the aftermath of the blast were only pieces of flesh and metal falling from the sky. The battle was finally over. But not without losses. Ryu was in a fight for his life. Maki ran over to Sarge and said. "You ain't dead, are you? "Sarge answered. "Hell no, I ain't dead, wise up boy."

"I did that so you'd finally ball up."

"Good to know you were faking it," Maki said, laughing.

Meanwhile, as Maki and Sarge celebrate their victory over Adam Shin, the twins, and Kagome run through the city streets, trying to get Ryu to Sakura before he succumbs to his injuries.

"If we can get him to the shrine in time, we can save him. Says Hariko, holding up his legs. Just then, a dark figure appears from the night fog. Watching them from a distance. They got to the shrine as Sakura was just getting out of bed from all the chaotic noises that emanated from the night. As the crew gets to her, she sees Ryu bleeding and unresponsive. She wasted no time running over to help.

"What the hell happened to him? Who did this?" asked Sakura.

"Death came knocking, and we answered the door," said Kagome. Using her blood manipulation skills, she stopped the bleeding, but he had lost too much blood and was fading fast. Just then, the figure came out of the darkness, revealing himself.

Death had come for Ryu.

CHAPTER 9
FAMILY

As the Yamato family tried to save Ryu, Death lurked in the background, waiting for his time to strike and collect his prize. Just then, Maki and Sarge arrived at the scene. And to Maki's surprise, he could see the grim reaper watching them from the darkness.

"Who the fuck is that?" Asked Maki

"Who?" Asked Sakura.

"The goth kid in the corner over there."

Death looked at Maki and laughed.

"You can finally see me. Impressive." Said Death. "But it doesn't matter if you can or not. The boy comes back with me."

"The hell he is," Maki says as he lunges at Death, but to no avail. Death turns into a black fog and dodges Maki's attacks. He then covers Ryu'''s body, smothering him and killing him slowly.

"Let him go!! Take me instead!" yelled Maki

"I already tried multiple times but failed each time. But your family was a good consolation prize."

"What you just say?" asked Maki

"Since I couldn't have you from the cancer so, I decided to take your whole family. I couldn't have your mother curing cancer now, could I?"

Maki screamed out in rage. "Come face me if you want me dead so badly."

"No, I'll be fine taking your adopted brother," said Death as he ripped the soul out of Ryu and finished him off.

"This isn't over," proclaimed Maki. "I'll find a way to make you pay."

"I'll be waiting." said Death as he slipped into the darkness.

Death had come for the fire bender, and there was nothing Maki could do to stop him. The thought of Death taking his friend consumed him. He spent his life searching for a way to enter the afterlife, where he hoped to find his loved ones and confront the Grim Reaper.

One day, he met Jazmine, a powerful young witch who claimed she could open a portal to the other side. She claimed to have given the clan the anonymous email that warned the crew of Adam's arrival. She was intrigued by Maki's story and agreed to help him, but only if he promised to do something for her in return. She did not reveal what it was, but Maki was desperate and accepted her offer.

Together with the Yamato clan, Jazmine and Maki had many adventures fighting off demons, ghouls, and ghosts, always protecting each other and watching each other's back. As time passed, Maki grew fond of Jazmine until the day came when it was time to confront Death on his own ground—the afterlife.

They traveled to a hidden cave, where Jazmine drew a circle of runes and candles on the ground. She told Maki to stand in the center and hold her hand. She began to chant in an ancient language, and the circle glowed with a dark light. Maki felt a strange sensation as if an invisible force was pulling him. He looked at Jazmine, who smiled and said, "Don't be afraid. We're almost there."

Suddenly, the circle exploded, and Maki felt a sharp pain in his chest. He looked down and saw a dagger plunged into his heart. He gasped and fell to his knees, blood spilling from his wound. He glanced at Jazmine, who had a twisted grin on her face. She said, "I'm sorry, Maki. But this was the only way. You see, I need your immortal soul to power my spell. It's the key to opening the portal. And don't worry, you'll still get to see your family and friends. In fact, they're waiting for you on the other side, along with death. He's been expecting you for a long time. Goodbye, Maki. And thank you for your sacrifice."

 She pulled the dagger out of his chest and stabbed it into the ground, completing the circle. A black hole opened in the air, and a cold wind blew from it. Maki felt his life fading away and his vision blurred. He heard a voice in his ear, a voice he recognized. It was his friend Ryu.

She used you, Maki. She's evil. She's the real threat. You have to stop her. You have to avenge us. Please, Maki. Please."

Maki felt a surge of anger and determination. He was not going to die like this. He was not going to let Jazmine get away with her crimes. He was not going to give up on his revenge. He gathered his last strength and crawled towards the portal. He reached out his hand and touched the edge of the hole. He felt a shock, and then he was gone.

He entered the afterlife, where he saw his family and friends waiting for him. They hugged him and cried and told him they loved him. They also told him the truth about Jazmine. How she was in a death cult and how she had been killing immortals for centuries, using their souls to fuel her dark magic. They said she was planning to utilize the portal to get her hands on the armor of the gods. The only thing that could kill a celestial being may be demonic or angelic. And if death gets his hands on the armor, a dark age of evil would encompass the world, and only Maki could stop her. They said they would help him and that they would fight by his side. They said they were proud of him and that they believed in him.

Maki smiled and thanked them. He felt a warmth in his heart and a peace in his mind. He also felt a fire in his eyes and a steel in his spine. He was ready. He turned around and faced the portal. He saw Jazmine standing on the other side, holding the dagger. She looked shocked and furious. She said, "Maki, you fool. How did you survive? How did you cross over? It's impossible. It's not fair. You're mine. You belong to me. Give me your soul. Give it to me now."

Maki said, "No, Jazmine. You're wrong. I don't belong to you. I belong to myself. And I belong to them. My family. My friend. They're my soul. And you can't have them. You can't have anything. You're done, Jazmine. You're finished. It's over. It's time to pay for what you've done. It's time to face death. And death is me."

He raised his hand and clenched his fist. He felt a power coursing through his veins, a power he had never felt before. He realized it was the power of life, the power of immortality. He said, "Jazmine, this is the end. This is your end. And this is my story. The story of Maki, the immortal with a personal vendetta with death. And this is how it ends."

He made a fist, and with his soul powers, he punched the ground, creating a shockwave, cracking the ground and collapsing the portal. Jazmine screamed, and then she was gone. Maki smiled, and then he was gone. They had returned to the afterlife, where his family and friends welcomed him. They cheered and celebrated, and then they embraced. They said, "Maki, you did it. You saved us. You're a hero, Maki. You're our hero. We love you, Maki. We love you so much."

Maki said, "I love you, too. I love you all. And I'm happy. I'm finally excited. I'm free. I'm free of death. I'm free of Jazmine. I'm free of pain. I'm free of hate. I'm free of fear.

But it's not over yet. Not until I stop Death from getting his hands on the armor. And so, Maki headed off to stop death from getting the armor of the gods. But not before his family bestowed upon him the mystical dragon armor, which allowed Maki to control his dragon form easily. He was one with the eternal dragon within.

Power radiated within him. He felt stronger than he'd ever felt before. "All of this has been a plan to get this armor, and I'll make sure none of them have it." Said Maki with determination in his voice. And so Maki made his way through the afterlife, looking for the armor.

Time moved differently in the afterlife, as one day in our world was ten years there. Maki searched for years, looking for the armor. He faced multiple creatures and demons in his search, defeating them all and becoming stronger with every battle.

Finally, he found the gateway to hell. He knew the armor was there from tips and stories told by the lost souls in the afterlife. He steadied himself as he walked through the gates into the fiery realm.

 As he entered, he saw a multitude of lost souls damned for eternity. Just then, he heard a familiar voice. It was Kenshin screaming in agony from the flames which engulfed him. Maki, he yelled out. "Maki, help me. Help me, my boy, please."

Good to see you, Uncle Kenshin. Maki said with a smile on his face.

"Looks like fate took care of you, huh, uncle?"

'Fate be damned… help me, boy!!!"

Maki goes into his travel pouch and pulls out a water bottle.

"Here, Uncle, this should help…" Maki says as he walks away.

"Now burn for your crimes, old man."

Maki walks away, showing no compassion for the evil scientist. He walks until a giant demonic creature stops him. He towered over Maki.

"Where are you going, mortal?" Asked the demon.

"I'm looking for the armor of the gods." He exclaimed.

The demon laughed at Maki, saying. "None have entered the chamber in which Lucifer resides and returned. Do you not value your soul?"

"I'm not like other mortals. I will return with the armor in hand," said Maki Confidently. With that, the demon laughed.

"Very well, mortal, you may pass. This will be entertaining." said the demon.

As he walked through the door, he wondered what evils were in store for him. What evil was awaiting him? He clenched his fists and entered the chamber of Lucifer. It was time for him to come face to face with the king of darkness. How would he handle this situation?

CHAPTER 10
GODS

As Maki entered the chamber of Lucifer, he steadied himself for whatever evils awaited him. To his surprise, the chamber was huge and vast. Going out as far as the eye can see. Just then, the memories of his school mythology classes returned to him. He realized that he was in the ancient realm of Tartarus. He saw Titans chained to the ground and fallen angels flying in the sky... It was terrifying and beautiful at the same time. Both fire and ice covered the landscape.

Just then, Maki heard a voice calling to him. "Free me." The voice begged. "Free me, and I'll make all of your dreams come true, mortal."

"Who are you?" Asked Maki.

"My name is Prometheus."

"Wait a minute. You're 'THE' Prometheus?" Asked Maki.

"Like the one that made us and gave us fire?"

"It is true I defied the gods and bestowed upon man fire, but for my supposed crimes, I've been trapped here in Tartarus for an eternity. Free me and receive your prize."

"All I want is information about the armor of the gods." Said Maki. "very well, I will tell you the history of the armor." said Prometheus

"First of all, it's not the armor of the gods. It's the Titan armor made of the very bones of Cronus, king of the Titans and master of time."

"It has the scales of the eternal dragon Bahamut, the black dragon. god of the dragons." With these scales, it can manipulate magic and all forms of energy. God-level magics would be children playing with the armor.

"It can control time and kill both Gods and Titans alike. It is the most deadly weapon in the cosmos. It was fashioned to absorb any energy, whether magical or elemental in nature.

It has within it the eye of Odin and the eye of Ra powering it. The eye of Odin gives it the power of Divine visions and gives the wielder the ability to see through the veil of time."

The eye of Ra grants the wielder resistance to any physical attacks by erecting impenetrable force fields and imbuing the wielder with unlimited strength, stamina, and durability.

Whoever wields the armor will be the most powerful being in the cosmos. A threat to any celestial beings. It could even kill death itself.

When Prometheus said that, it rang in Maki's brain. "Kill death, you say?" Maki asked. "And what would happen if I were to kill death?"

"The fates would choose a new death to replace this one. The world must know death."

"Now I have told you all I know of this. Now release me." Maki took his blade from his sheath, and using his dragon form, he cut through the chains, releasing Prometheus. The Titan stood tall for the first time in a millennium. "Thank you, mortal," he exclaimed. "For your good deed, I will show you where the armor is being held. But be wary, for it is not easy to claim it once you find it."

"Don't you worry about that," said Maki. I'll take care of Lucy; you just get me to that armor."

And so, Prometheus took him to a distant cave surrounded by fire and ice. It looked like something was absorbing the elements into the cave like a vacuum.

"This is as far as I go." Said Prometheus. "I just got my freedom, and I intend to use it. But whenever you need, call me, and I'll be there to assist you."

They shook hands, and Maki entered the cave. As he walked through the cave, he noticed men, women, and demons alike frozen around the cave, like statues all around him. These beings were unfortunate enough to get too close to the armor and had their souls ripped out of their bodies. Then, as he walked deeper into the cave, he felt the pull of the armor. Luckily, his immortal body was strong enough to withstand the soul-draining effects of the armor. It led him directly to it.

The armor was in front of him, hanging on the far side of the cave wall. As he approached the armor, he felt a cold presence watching him from the darkness. Suddenly, a large demon arose from the very shadows on the ground. He was huge. He towered over Maki and said. Who dares enter my realm?

With no hesitation, Maki runs past the demon for the armor, just to be grabbed in mid-air by the demon's claws. He slammed Maki into the ground and followed by spewing hot lava at the immortal. But Maki jumped out of the magma and kept trying to get to the armor, but to no avail. Every attack was countered, and every move was anticipated. Lucifer had Maki beaten. He picks up Maki and attempts to eat him whole. But Maki comes down onto the monster's head and stabs him in the eye.

Enraged, he rips Maki in two, throwing one half away and devouring the other. But the upper half of Maki is still moving. He crawls with all he has to the armor. He touches it with his bloody hand and then passes out.

"Noo!!" Exclaimed Lucifer as he flies towards the armor.

But it was too late. The armor had tasted the blood of a mortal and wanted more. The armor came to life, locking onto Maki's leftovers, rebuilding his body, and covering it with itself. The armor was absorbing Maki whole. Lucifer grabbed the armor and attempted to separate the two, but Maki severed Lucifer's hand just then. He falls into the lava. The armor is still combined with him. The armor took Maki whole. Metal and flesh are becoming one.

In moments, Maki arose from the magma, empowered by the armor. He looks over at Lucifer and teleports to him in an instant. With a backhand, he sends Lucifer into the wall.

"That's for being a crappy host. But I do not quarrel with you, so I'll let you live. But if I ever catch you in the mortal realm. I will kill you." Said Maki

"That armor was never to be worn, especially not by a mortal. It is too dangerous to be released into the world," said Lucifer

It's only dangerous for gods and your kind, but I'm a mortal so that I won't abuse my new powers. Said Maki. "I just want death."

"He's the only celestial I want dead. Now, where is he hiding? I know you know Lucy."

"You don't even know what you are now, do you, boy? When you put on that armor, you give up your mortality. You're a celestial being now. What a joke, a celestial being with a human soul. You have no place anywhere now, boy. Neither man nor God will accept you. You're an abomination of the cosmos." Said Lucifer

"Are you trying to piss me off, Lucy? Cuz it's working," said Maki as he conjured a fireball in his hand. Lucifer says, "No, just telling you what you have in store.

" Now, where is death?" Said Maki angrily. He's in the cemetery between worlds of life and death. He stays there next to his lover, the demon lord Lilith.

The cemetery, huh? He thinks back to the last time he went to the cemetery and the battle they waged there fighting Victor. "Ok, I'm on it."

"Say hello to Zeus for me," Lucifer says as Maki leaves the cave. "He'll definitely be calling you soon." And with that, Maki leaves the cave with the mystical armor in hand. As he left the cave, he felt a new sensation and attempted something that was just a

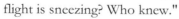

pipe dream. He tried to fly.

He jumped into the air but to no avail. He tried again, but nothing. Then, just as he was going to give up, he sneezed, propelling him back and into the air. "Seriously? He asks. "the secret to flight is sneezing? Who knew."

And with that, Maki practiced flying before darting

out into the air. The wind in his hair, the bugs in his face. It was glorious. Before he left the chambers, he wanted to try something. So, he closed his eyes and called upon Prometheus. In an instant, he appeared to Maki. "What is it you need?" Asked Prometheus. "I was wondering what you would do with your freedom." Asked Maki. "I don't know just yet. I still have to leave this place."

"I got you, bro." Said Maki. "You can come live with us at the dojo. All I ask is that you keep telling me what you know about stuff… knowledge is power, and you've seen it all."

"Fair enough, I'll take you up on that offer," said Prometheus

"The first thing I think I'll tell you is how to use your magic."

"Seriously?! Hellzyea!" Maki yelled out. And so, Maki learned as they made their way out of the chamber. But when they made it out, an army of demons was waiting for them. "Do you wanna do the honors?" said Prometheus. "Time to test this thing out." Maki stepped forward and conjured a scythe in his hands. "Leave or die. Your choice."

With that, the horde of demons attacked. As they swarmed Maki, he laid his hands down on the ground and conjured a magical circle around him, and with no magic, he summoned fire from the sky, bombarding the hundreds of demons. He then jumped into the middle of the swarm, slashing and cleaving the demons down. Then, with one word, "stone." He turned the Armies of the Damned into stone. Then, I proceeded to smash them one by one. "That was fun as hell," Maki exclaimed.

"Looked fun," said Prometheus as they continued past the rubble that was once the demon army. They made their way back to the mortal realm. Before Maki went to get his revenge, he wanted to make sure Prometheus was set up in his new home. Plus, Maki wanted to show Shin the armor. They landed in the Yamato family courtyard. Kimiko asks, "Were you just flying?"

"Yup!! Jealous much?" Said Maki.

"No. Not even," said Hariko as she wondered just how this was.

"Well, we can talk about this later. This is my new friend Prometheus, and he's cool as hell."

And with that, Prometheus started to live with the Yamato family as a spiritual advisor due to his knowledge of the cosmos. Together, they went on adventures and saved multiple people from demons, ghouls, and ghosts. But as time went by, Maki became distracted from his family's murder. But he trained himself in the mystical arts and mastered the armor, learning all he could from Prometheus. He was ready to bring the fight to death and finish it once and for all.

CHAPTER 11

THE TRIAL

Months had passed since Maki returned with Prometheus from the other side, and the city had become much safer. The twins had the Slayers patrolling the city for supernatural creatures. Every night, Maki and Shin would go out to get their Batman and Robin on by protecting the citizens of Kyoto, one ghoul vampire or demon at a time. One night, they came across a lost little girl. Her name was Jade, and she was 12 years old. They found her outside of a vampire's den, about to be a midnight smack. She lost her sister months ago and was homeless. So, they brought her home to the Yamato family dojo. Maki saw her as a new little sister, and the twins instantly fell in love with her.

Months had passed, and Maki, Shin, and the crew were happy; they had a nice, happy new family. One night, an old man came knocking at the gate. Jade ran to the door, unaware of the dangers that lurked in the dark. She opened the door to find three ghastly creatures awaiting her. They grabbed the child and fled off into the night as Maki and Hariko watched in horror.

The entire clan went out searching for Jade, but by the time they found her, it was too late. The ghouls had already harvested her for her organs and were feeding.

The Slayers cared for the ghouls while Maki Shin and the rest mourned her loss. Just then, the Reaper returned to collect Jade's soul. Maki stood up, ready to fight the dark one-off, but that's when Prometheus stopped him. "If he doesn't take her now, she'll suffer from the wounds the ghouls bestowed upon her. Brother, let her go. if you love her, you must." Said Prometheus.

And so, he closed his eyes and allowed death to take her.

He loved her like his own flesh and blood, and he was devastated by her loss.

He decided to use his powers to track down the reaper and confront him in his realm once and for all. He knew it was a dangerous and reckless mission, but he didn't care. He wanted to make the reaper pay for what he had done. He gathered his weapons and relics and prepared to leave.

Before he left, he said goodbye to his master, Renjin, the head of the dojo and the only person who knew he was leaving. Renjin tried to dissuade him from going, but Maki was determined. He thanked him for everything he had taught and asked him to look after the dojo and the other students. He then opened a portal to the underworld and stepped through.

He arrived in a dark and gloomy place filled with bones, skulls, and tombstones. He felt a cold and oppressive aura and heard the cries and moans of the souls trapped there. He sensed the presence of the reaper and followed it. He soon found him sitting on a throne made of bones, holding a scythe in his hand. Ghouls, his loyal servants, surrounded him.

Maki wasted no time, and charged at him, shouting his name. The reaper looked up and smiled wickedly. He recognized Maki and said, "Ah, the immortal exorcist. I've been expecting you. You've been a nuisance to me for a long time. But today, you will meet your end."

He ordered his ghouls to attack Maki, and they obeyed. Maki fought them off, using his sword and his exorcism skills. He slashed, stabbed, and banished them, one by one. He made his way to the reaper, who watched him with amusement. He said, "You're wasting your time, Maki. You can't kill me. I am death itself. I am eternal. And you are nothing but a mortal who cheated death. You don't belong here. You don't belong anywhere."

Maki ignored him and reached him. He swung his sword at him, aiming for his neck. The reaper blocked it with his scythe and pushed him back. He said, "You're foolish, Maki. You think you can avenge your sister and family, but you can't. She was destined to die. It was her fate. And it is yours, too. You can't escape it. You can't escape me."

He swung his scythe at Maki, who dodged it. He said, "You're wrong, reaper. You're not fate. You're not justice. You're not a god. You're a monster. A tyrant. A murderer. You took my sister from me. You took my family. You took everything from me. And I will take everything from you."

He lunged at him and stabbed him in the chest. The reaper gasped and dropped his scythe. He looked at Maki and said, "How...how did you...?"

Maki said, "I told you, reaper. I'm an exorcist. I can banish anything. Even you."

He twisted his sword, and the reaper screamed. He exploded into dust, and his scythe fell to the ground. Maki picked it up and held it in his hand. He felt a surge of power and a voice in his head. It said, "Congratulations, Maki. You have defeated the reaper. You have inherited his power. You are the new God of death."

Maki was shocked and said, "What? No. I don't want this. I don't want to be like him."

The voice said, "You have no choice, Maki. This is your destiny. This is your curse. You are immortal, and you are dead. You will rule over the underworld and reap the souls of the living. You will be feared and hated by all. You will be alone and miserable. You will never see your sister again. You will never see anyone again. You will be the reaper."

Maki dropped the scythe and fell to his knees. He cried out, "No! No! No!"

He called out for Prometheus, and in minutes, he was there, shocked to see Maki on his knees crying.

"What happened? Where's death?" Asked Prometheus

"I killed him, and voices told me I was to be the new death."

"I can sense the presence of gods among us," Prometheus said as he turned around to see multiple deities appear from thin air.

"I'm not in the mood, guys. Go home now or die," said Maki angrily

"Oh, we're going home, but not alone." said one of the warriors

Just then, a bright light engulfed the group. Teleporting all of them to another realm. They were in New Olympus and surrounded by hundreds of warriors ready for battle.

"I don't know who you are or where we are, but I know what time it will be if any of you take that first step," Maki exclaimed. He then made a line in the dirt and dared any of them to cross. Just then, a large fireball came barreling through the sky. As it got closer, it transformed into a chariot. And upon the chariot was Apollo, the sun God.

"It's time for your trial, murderer," Apollo said, looking at Maki.

"Trial for what?" Asked Maki. You killed my uncle Hades, and now you'll pay for your crime. "If your uncle was the piece of shit, I just killed them. Yes, I killed him…and I'd kill him again if I could."

Those words enraged Apollo. He raised his hand and brought forth a large fireball to incinerate Maki. "That was a confession of guilt. You killed my uncle. Now you die."

"You don't wanna do that, Apollo." Said Prometheus.

"Silence, Titan dog! You'll be back in chains by nightfall. And you'll be dead!!"

With that, Apollo launches the fireball, hitting Maki dead. But to Apollo's surprise, he was unscathed. The Titan armor had protected him.

"My turn, bright boy." And with that, Maki said, "Burn," and a black fire tornado engulfed Apollo, nearly burning him to a crisp.

"Enough!!" yelled a voice from the sky as lightning rang through the air. Zeus had arrived and was wondering what the hell was going on.

"I sent the advanced guard to bring the new death to the palace, not to kill him." "But he killed Lord Hades," argued Apollo. "Enough of your excuses.

Now leave me." With that, Apollo disappeared in flames. Now, shall we go to the palace and discuss your new position? Asked Zeus

"We shall not thunder butt," Maki said defiantly.

"Thunder butt? "Asked Zeus. "Well, if not the palace, then the dungeon." And with that, Maki was struck down by a multitude of lightning bolts, stunning him and knocking him unconscious.

When Maki awoke, he was in the dungeon covered in chains. He tried to break them but to no avail.

"Those chains were made by Hephaestus. You can't break them, friend," said Prometheus.

 "Where are we? Disney World?" "I wish. We're in the dungeon of new Olympus."

"Our trial is in the morning, so get some sleep."

"I've gotta plan." Said Maki.

"Plan? What plan?" Said Prometheus

"Don't worry, I got this," exclaimed Maki.

The next day, the trial began, and within minutes of opening arguments, Maki demanded to be heard. He looked at Zeus and challenged all of the gods to trial by combat. Zeus was intrigued by the concept and agreed to the terms.

If Maki won, he was granted one request, but if he lost, he would be banished to Tartarus to rule over the dead for eternity. It was to be a one-on-one fight between a god and a mortal. Not since Hercules had a mortal tested the gods. Maki steadied himself as trumpets blew in the colosseum as the warrior of the gods made his way to the battlefield.

It was Apollo revitalized and ready for battle. He descended from the heavens like a hawk descended upon his prey. He was ready for battle. He was ready for revenge. He was ready for Maki this time. He looked at the crowd and dedicated the fight to Hades, the former God of death. The crowd cheered with anticipation for the bloodshed.

A loud gong went off, signaling the beginning of the battle. The two deities clashed in mid-air. Their powers radiated off each other as the crowd went wild. They exchanged blows as the sky was filled with fire and lightning.

"You're better than I expected," said Apollo.

"Same to you." Maki Said with respect in his voice.

"It's a shame I'll have to kill you."

And with that, Maki backhanded the God, crashing him down into the ground and following up with a thunderous elbow drop, inflicting damage on the God. He stood up and kicked Apollo in the chest, sending him crashing into the wall. He watched as Apollo crawled out of the rubble, ready for round 2.

Apollo summoned a fire spirit to incinerate Maki, but as the creature approached Maki, he just batted it away with a simple gesture of his hand.

Is that your best? Maki asked as the flames disappeared in his wake. Apollo, furious, attempts to summon the very sun to burn Maki then and there, but Maki isn't playing that game. He teleports to Apollo, stopping the spell with a swift and powerful punch to the abdomen. He then spin-kicks him, sending him flying back once again. Enraged, Apollo takes out a large dagger to kill Maki once and for all. The crowd explodes when they see the blade.

"Finish him." says the audience. "Kill the mortal!"

Then Apollo transformed into pure fire and launched himself at Maki, attacking the immortal with all his godly power.

But Maki isn't fazed in the least. He jumps into the air and clutches his fist. With a loud boom, Maki slams into the earth, causing a massive earthquake and slowing Apollo down long enough for him to hit him with a flying knee strike, turning him back into his humanoid form.

Apollo swings the dagger and attacks Maki, but Maki grabs the blade, shoving it into the chest of God, stopping him in his tracks. Apollo drops to one knee. The crowd falls silent as Apollo draws his last breath.

As Apollo dies in Maki's arms, the sun blackens, and thunder rings out throughout the realm. Zeus stands at attention as Apollo falls to the ground. The eternal glow of Apollo's light dimmed and faded away. The sun turned black as onyx. Maki felt another surge of power engulf him. Maki had won the contest, but a mysterious figure jumped into the arena and charged at Maki at full speed.

Maki ducks and dodges the attacks, then pushes away the assailant. "Ok, now, who the fuck is you?!"

Maki asked.

The man stands upright and says. "I am the God of war, Ares, and you are an immortal. The contest was rigged from the beginning. His pride weakened Apollo, and he wasn't ready for this kind of battle. But I am."

"God of war, you say?" Maki asks. "Well, let's see what the 'god of war' can do. Come at me, bro. With everything you've got. Or you'll die like the sun God here." With that, the two clashed. Maki is holding his own against the war god. Sparks flew as their swords clashed. They battled for what seemed like an eternity. Neither one is giving an inch. Ares hits Maki with a devastating kick to the head, spilling him around them and hitting him with a large fireball. Maki comes back with a thunderous headbutt to the head, making Ares bleed out. He then jumps into the air and attacks Ares with a cleaving blow, which slices him in two.

Zeus jumps out of his seat and into the arena. "What have you done?!" Yelled Zeus.

"I just killed another God who doesn't know their place." Exclaimed Maki." I wield the Titan armor, and I take a god's powers with every kill. I have the powers of the sun God, the God of death, and now... the God of war. I feel their power radiating within me. And Now you can be the next old man.

He finally reached the throne of Zeus, the king of the gods, who wielded the mighty thunderbolt. Maki challenged him to a final battle, with the crown of the gods as the prize. Zeus accepted, confident in his supremacy. The two immortals clashed in a fierce and epic combat, shaking the heavens and the earth. They exchanged blows and blasts, each one trying to overpower the other. Maki dodged and parried the thunderbolts while Zeus blocked and countered the attacks of Maki's divine arsenal. The fight lasted for days and nights until both of them were exhausted and wounded.

Maki saw an opening and lunged at Zeus, stabbing him in the chest with a sword he had taken from Ares, the god of war. Zeus gasped and dropped his thunderbolt, which Maki quickly grabbed and aimed at his head. He pulled the trigger, unleashing a massive bolt of lightning that struck Zeus in the forehead, killing him instantly. Maki stood over the fallen king of the gods, holding the thunderbolt in his hand. He had done it. He had defeated all the gods in his way. He had become the king of the gods.

He felt a surge of triumph and joy but also a pang of sadness and emptiness. He realized he had nothing left to do, nothing left to strive for, nothing left to live for. He had reached the end of his journey but also lost his way. He wondered if this was his curse: to be immortal but unhappy, powerful but alone, King but not God. He looked at the thunderbolt, the symbol of his victory and his folly, and made a decision. He turned it towards himself and pressed the trigger.

But to no surprise, he could not die. He arose bewildered at why he would have tried that. A voice rings in his head...try again.

"Wait, who are you?" Maki thought to himself.

"I am Chronos." the voice answers. "I'm the reason you're King. I'm the one that gave you the ability to kill gods. And I am the one who shall rule."

"You've got it all wrong, bro. My name is Maki, and I am the immortal. So that means you're stuck in here with me for the long haul." Says Maki

And so, Maki, using the armor, floats up to the throne and takes his well-earned seat upon it. He thought of his parents, and he thought of his loved ones. He wondered if he'd ever see them again.

Heavy is the head that holds the crown. For now, he was the king "IN HEAVEN AND HELL."

CHAPTER 12
KING

He had left the world below him. After defeating Zeus in a fierce battle, he had been the king of Olympus for a few months. He had inherited the power and responsibility of ruling over the gods and the underworld but also felt lonely.

He missed his mortal life, his adopted family, and friends from the Yamato clan, who had trained him in martial arts and taught him / the values of honor and loyalty. He missed the simple joys of eating, drinking, laughing, and fighting with them. He missed the dojo, where he had spent many hours honing his skills and learning from his master, Renjin sensei.

He wondered how they were doing, if they were still alive and well if they remembered him. He wished he could see them again, even for a moment. He longed for the mortal world, a world he had left behind when he ascended to Olympus.

He decided to act on his impulse. He got up from his throne, put on a cloak to disguise his divine aura, and headed to the portal that connected Olympus to the world. He told no one of his plan, not even his loyal companion, Prometheus, the Titan. He wanted to surprise his old friends, and he also wanted to avoid any interference from the other gods, who might not approve of his visit.

He stepped into the portal and felt a rush of air and light. He emerged in a forest near the Yamato clan's territory. He recognized the place; he had been there before. He smiled and started to walk towards the dojo, hoping to find his family and friends there. He hoped they would be happy to see him and not be afraid of his new status. He hoped they would still accept him as one of them, as Maki.

But when he arrived at the dojo, all that was left was a smoldering pile of ash. The dojo had been burned to the ground. Who, how, when, all these questions ran through Maki's mind.

"I told you that you were all alone now," said Chronos

"Quiet down, Chronos. I'm trying to think." Who could've done this to them, he wondered. Perhaps Prometheus knew something about it. So, he closed his eyes and summoned Prometheus to him.

"My lord," Prometheus exclaimed

"Quit that 'lord' crap, and just tell me what happened here. Who did this to our family? Our friends?" Asked Maki

"I don't know, but I know how to find out," said Prometheus.

"You're the key, Maki. You are one with the Titan armor and the Titan of Time Chronos. You can look through the veil of time and space. You can see all past and most future events. Just concentrate, and you can see what happened with your eyes."

So, Maki closed his eyes and called upon the powers of Chronos, the Titan of time. Energy surrounded him as the veil of time opened in front of him. He opened his eyes to see the dojo under attack by demons. He watched as the demon legions swarmed the city and assaulted the dojo.

"Where are they coming from?" asked Maki

"Your foolishness knows no bounds, boy," said Chronos

"They came from the hole you left in Tartarus as you left."

This is all your fault."

"No, it can't be true. I won't accept this. I can't accept this." he said as he stressed over the words that came from Chronos. I must make it right. I must save them. Save them from my mistake. With that, he summoned the sands of time. The sands circled and engulfed him, sending him flying back into the past. But he had never attempted to travel through time, so he overshot his destination and landed in Kyoto months before the attack. He decides to stay in this timeline because time traveling back and forth might cause some damage to the flow of time.

He went to the clan dojo doors to see Kimiko and

Hariko working on a new experiment. He ran to them, holding them close to him. Tears ran down his eyes. "I promise I'll never leave you guys again," Maki said, crying. This sensitive side of Maki was new to the girls and kind of freaked them out. They called Sarge to see what's going on with Maki.

"You good boy? "Asked Sarge

"Yeah, I just had a really long day," said Maki.

He calls Prometheus to him and asks. Do you know?

"Yes, I can sense the presence of the sands about you. You've time traveled, but I must ask why when you should know the risk."

"Soon, all of them will die, and I won't allow it!" Said Maki

"Ok, that's all you had to say. I've grown fond of the Yamato family, and we won't allow any bloodshed of the clan or anyone else."

With that, Maki and Prometheus began protecting the Yamato family and the surrounding city. But Maki didn't stop with just protection. He started Shin on a new training regimen that would unlock all of his hidden abilities. They trained daily to master Shin's lightning bolts to the point that Maki said he was a rival to Zeus himself.

Then, one night, a beautiful woman came knocking on the door. Her hair was as red as fire, and her beauty was unmatched by normal standards. She asked to speak to Maki directly.

As Maki made his way to the door, a strange sensation took him over. The feeling of murderous intent filled the air. He approached the woman and asked who she was.

"My name is Lilith." And with that, the ground started to quake. "I was death's lover until you took him away from me. Now I take from you."

Maki took his stance, ready to go to war. It was here the night he'd prepared for. The fall of the Yamato family dojo was upon them. Thousands of demons then arose out of the shadows of the city.

But the crew was ready; the twins had made multiple new Slayers in response to talking with Maki earlier. Sarge was also prepared as the werewolf equipped himself with grenade launchers and chainsaws, ready for the long battle ahead. Shin stood ready with twin lightning katana blades. And even Sakura was ready on the roof with her sniper rifle, ready to take out the legions of demons one bullet at a time. Kagome summoned a strong, freezing wind, which froze the demons in place momentarily so that Sarge could blow them away with his grenade launchers. Maki summoned the armies of Olympus to assist with the battle. And so, the battle lines were set. The largest battle of good vs evil had begun. But who would win? The evil of the underworld or the powers of good led by Maki and Shin?

As the battle began, you could tell Maki had changed the Olympian army to fit the times as they came in, not finishing swords and shields but AR-15s and rocket launchers. In the span of a few months, Maki had the Olympian army ready to take on the residents of hell. They showered the legions of demons with bullets fabricated by the Renjin Sensei. They used magically infused weaponry to cut down the ground forces of the underworld, but just then, a giant demon appeared on the battlefield. He swung a mighty Axe and sword, cleaving through the soldiers. He spat hot lava from his mouth.

"That one Is mine," said Sarge as he grabbed the chain grenade launcher from his pouch. I jumped on a motorcycle and hit the road. Laughing aloud while blasting music, he spins around the legs of the demonic force, firing off the chain grenade launcher and wrapping up the legs of the beast. He then detonates the grenades all at once, bringing the beast to his knees. He turned, did a wheelie jump, and with the motorcycle, leaped off and, with his razor-sharp claws, beheads the demon in one swing.

Kagome then summons a small army of Frost golems to the battle. They jump right into the swarm of demons, swinging giant clubs and batting demons away like flies. She then summons a blizzard to engulf the whole city. The wind blows with no remorse as the cold freezes the demonic army in its tracks. She uses her ice skates to descend upon the battlefield, shattering every demon in her way. Sakura then fires her 50-caliber tank buster sniper rifle at one of the giant demons frozen on the field, shattering it.

The Slayers took to the sky and destroyed all aerial threats. Blasting the winged demons out of the sky and bombarding ground forces.

Meanwhile, back at the dojo, Maki and Shin are battling Lilith, Lord of the demons. She is quick and agile, and Shin and Maki couldn't get close enough to lay the killing blow.

"They may call you king, but you fight like a child," said Lilith

"Of course, I'm a kid to an old bitch like you.! What are you really? Are you really 2 or maybe 3 million years old? "

"Must be screwing death. I mean, death? Really?"

This enraged Lilith, making her radiate with energy. She pulls out a chain whip to punish Maki for his words. For his disrespectful tone and for sweet Hades, which he had taken from her.

And so, Lilith Maki and Shin battled her speed being an issue for Maki and Shin, even at top speed. At the speed of light, they couldn't land the final blow.

"You just don't know how to fight like a good boy," said Chronos. "If I were fighting her, she'd be long dead at my feet.

"You're right," Maki said to himself as he stopped chasing Lilith. I just need this. He then summons the powers of all the deities he's tested and defeated, starting with Hades. He raised his hand, and a black orb arose from his palm. The orb flew high into the sky and then erupted in a wave of black energy, hitting every demon within a 10-mile radius, killing them all instantly but not injuring any of their allies.

"The death nukes. Like it?"

Lilith sensed the death of over 90% of her forces. "Bastards!!"

Maki looked at Shin and said. "Go check on the crew, bro…. I got this from here. He smiled at Shin, saying. "I need to go god mode, but I can't with you here."

"Okay, brother, just kill the bitch. Good, okay."

"I got you."

And so, Maki turned around and faced Lilith, the demonic goddess. He called upon the sword of Ares, the flames of Apollo, and the thunderbolts of Zeus combined. Power radiated from Maki. Fire and lightning engulfed him. The blade glowed red with energy and heat.

He was ready. Lilith spreads her wings, revealing a twin-spiked Bo staff. "Do you know what this is?" asked Lilith. "It's the spear of destiny. I've had it for a millennium, and now it will drink of your blood. The only other thing that can kill a god. Shall we dance together for one last time?

"The two clashed, moving at light speed across the city and landscape until they found themselves high in orbit. Lilith raises her spear to the sky and summons forth a creature from another dimension to eat Maki. He dodges the large beast mid-air, spinning and diving in the air. He stops and asks himself if he should use 'that' spell, but then he decides as the creature approaches. He puts his hand upon the earth and says, "Come forth, Bahamut!"

And with that, the dragon god was released from his prison. With one clean motion, the god of dragons grabs the lesser beast by its neck and easily rips its head off, spewing blood and magma everywhere. He then looks at Maki, then Lilith, and Maki gives the orders. "Kill her, boy." Bahamut then opens his mouth to unleash a black plasma attack. He powers it up and fires as Lilith jumps out of the way. But then runs right into Maki barreling down upon her. He swings his flaming sword, cleaving through her neck and decapitating her. He then grabbed her limp body and threw it to BAHAMUT to eat as a sign of goodwill to the dragon god. he grabbed her head and tossed it into space to float amongst the stars forevermore. It was over, but now what? Kyoto is in ruins, and there is a hole in the veil that separates earth and hell, and he must fix it. But how?

He flew back down, seeing the last few demons scurry away into the darkness. With a sigh of relief, Maki returned to the dojo to access the casualty reports. To make sure no one was lost. But to his surprise, none of the Yamato family had been injured. All were in good health. Maki knew it would be a long road rebuilding the city, but with the Olympian army, it took less than one year for Kyoto to be bigger and better than ever.

When Kyoto was rebuilt, and the Yamato family was honored for their contributions to the battle, it came to Maki to say goodbye. It was time for him to take his place as ruler. He hugged his loved ones, the Yamato family and friends, and headed off. But not before giving Shin a magical bell. "Ring these three times, and I'll be there anytime, anywhere," said Maki as he hugged his adopted brother. And with that, he left to reign over the heavens and hell. He would do whatever it takes to protect our world from the darkness that comes from both heaven and hell. He wouldn't stop. He'd never give up. He'd be watching over us for all of eternity. And with that, a new constellation was born. It was named the immortal in honor of Maki. The sick Little boy who had become a God and saved us all.

The end.

Made in the USA
Columbia, SC
29 July 2024

39632208R00054